Dear Parents:

Congratulations! Your child is taking the first steps on an exciting journey. The destination? Independent reading!

STEP INTO READING® will help your child get there. The program offers five steps to reading success. Each step includes fun stories and colorful art or photographs. In addition to original fiction and books with favorite characters, there are Step into Reading Non-Fiction Readers, Phonics Readers and Boxed Sets, Sticker Readers, and Comic Readers—a complete literacy program with something to interest every child.

Learning to Read, Step by Step!

Ready to Read   Preschool–Kindergarten
• big type and easy words • rhyme and rhythm • picture clues
For children who know the alphabet and are eager to begin reading.

Reading with Help   Preschool–Grade 1
• basic vocabulary • short sentences • simple stories
For children who recognize familiar words and sound out new words with help.

Reading on Your Own   Grades 1–3
• engaging characters • easy-to-follow plots • popular topics
For children who are ready to read on their own.

Reading Paragraphs   Grades 2–3
• challenging vocabulary • short paragraphs • exciting stories
For newly independent readers who read simple sentences with confidence.

Ready for Chapters   Grades 2–4
• chapters • longer paragraphs • full-color art
For children who want to take the plunge into chapter books but still like colorful pictures.

STEP INTO READING® is designed to give every child a successful reading experience. The grade levels are only guides; children will progress through the steps at their own speed, developing confidence in their reading.

Remember, a lifetime love of reading starts with a single step!

Step into Reading, Random House, and the Random House colophon are registered trademarks of Penguin Random House LLC.

Visit us on the Web!
StepIntoReading.com
rhcbooks.com

Educators and librarians, for a variety of teaching tools, visit us at RHTeachersLibrarians.com

ISBN 978-0-525-58058-4 (trade) — ISBN 978-0-525-58059-1 (lib. bdg.) — ISBN 978-0-525-64452-1 (ebook)

Printed in the United States of America

10 9 8 7 6 5 4 3 2 1

ILLUMINATION PRESENTS

Dr. Seuss'

The **GRINCH**

WELCOME TO WHO-VILLE

by Mary Tillworth

illustrated by Shane Clester

Random House 🏠 New York

All the Whos
are excited.
Christmas is coming
to Who-ville!

4

Cindy-Lou
is bold and brave.
She likes to
go on adventures.
Cindy-Lou loves
Christmas.
She wants to meet
Santa Claus in person.

Groopert wears

a blue and white scarf.

He has curly red hair.

Groopert and Cindy-Lou
are best friends.
When Cindy-Lou
makes a plan,
she always calls Groopert!

Izzy wears earmuffs
to keep her ears warm.
Ozzy's goggles stop the wind
from getting into his eyes.

Axl looks good
in his blue coat.
When Cindy-Lou needs help,
she can always count
on her friends!

Donna is Cindy-Lou's mom.
She loves her children
very much.
Donna looks forward to
spending Christmas
with her family.

Bricklebaum is
the Grinch's neighbor.
He has a big bushy beard.
He wears a red sweater
with pine trees on it.

Bricklebaum is jolly and kind.
He might love Christmas
more than any
other Who!

Up in the hills
lives the Grinch.
The Grinch is
tall and green
and lonely and mean.
His heart is two sizes
too small.
He doesn't like
Christmas at all!

Max lives
with the Grinch.
He has long fluffy ears
and a fluffy tail, too.
Max is the Grinch's
best friend.

Fred is a big reindeer.

He has short antlers.

He becomes friends

with the Grinch and Max.

Uh-oh!

The Grinch has a plan.

He will steal Christmas

from the Whos!

But Cindy-Lou
and the other Whos
teach the Grinch to
love Christmas.

Together, the Whos
and the Grinch celebrate
Christmas!

Merry Christmas!